# The Pizza Princess

Written by Miriam Simon
Illustrated b

Once upon a time there was a princess.

She ate pizza for breakfast,

pizza for lunch

and pizza for tea.

Every day she shouted,
'I want a pizza!'

Then the maid ran to the cook,
the cook made the pizza
and the princess ate it.

Every night she shouted,
'I want a pizza!'
The maid ran to the cook,
the cook made the pizza
and the princess ate it.

But one day, the princess shouted,
'I want a pizza!'
And nothing happened.

She looked everywhere.
There was no maid.
There was no cook

and there was no pizza.
The princess cried.

Then she looked out of the window.

There was the cook.
There was the maid.
And there was the pizza . . .
in a new pizza palace!

The new pizza palace was full of people.
The people didn't shout.
They said, 'Pizza please,' very quietly.

The cook was happy
and the maid was happy.
The princess was sad.

'I want a pizza!' she shouted.
But nothing happened.

The princess got very thin.

Then, one day, she went to
the new pizza palace.

She said, very quietly,
'I want a pizza . . .

please.'

The maid ran to the cook.
The cook made the pizza
and the princess said, 'Thank you.'

Everybody was happy.
And the princess ate pizza every day.